To my loving wife.

There is nothing

common

about you.

WHISPERS
OF THE
ELDORIAN CRYSTAL

PATH OF THE
COMMONER

WHISPERS OF THE ELDORIAN CRYSTAL

PATH OF THE COMMONER

A Pick•Your•Path•Adventure

Eric Johnson

Broken Table
Press

First printing, 2024.

Broken Table Press
Belchertown, MA, 01007

ISBN 978-1-7362707-6-9

www.ericjohnsonwriter.com

PRINTED IN THE UNITED STATES OF AMERICA

Your story begins

As you stand at the edge of the Enchanted Forest of Eldoria, a gentle breeze rustles the leaves above you, carrying with it whispers of ancient magic. The tall trees loom like sentinels, their branches reaching out as if to beckon you into their mysterious depths. Sunlight dances through the canopy, casting dappled patterns on the forest floor where colorful flowers bloom in abundance.

In the distance, you hear the faint trill of a bird and the soft gurgle of a hidden stream. The air is sweet with the scent of wildflowers and earth, filling your senses with a heady mix of wonder and excitement. Your heart races with the promise of adventure, and your curiosity burns bright like a flame within you.

As you turn away from the Enchanted Forest of Eldoria, your eyes fall upon the quaint village of Meadowfen

behind you. The cobblestone streets wind through the heart of the settlement, lined with colorful houses adorned with blooming window boxes overflowing with vibrant flowers. Tucked back among the cobblestones is your cottage, your mother probably baking her famous bustle berry pie. The warm glow of lanterns illuminates the path ahead, casting a soft, inviting light on the cozy scene before you.

The inviting aroma of freshly baked bread wafts through the air, intermingling with the scent of wood smoke from chimneys. Laughter and chatter drift from open windows, accompanied by the gentle melody of a lute played by a talented minstrel in the town square. Children run through the fields behind you, their joyful squeals filling the air as they play games of tag amongst themselves.

You catch sight of your friends gathered under the old oak tree near the fountain at the heart of the village, one of many such groups preparing for the upcoming races. They wave excitedly as they spot you, beckoning you to join them with joyful shouts. "Come join us!" calls out your best friend, Sariah, her bright eyes shining with anticipation of the upcoming Starlight Races.

Join Sariah and your friends. (Go to page 3)

Ignore the calls and enter the forest. (Go to page 5)

Join Sariah and your friends.

As dusk falls over Meadowfen, the village hums with excitement. Tonight is the night of the Starlight Races, a time when the fields and forests come alive with the glow of Eldorian fireflies. You've been looking forward to this night for weeks, and as the sun dips below the horizon, painting the sky in shades of purple and orange, you feel a tingle of magic in the air.

You meet your best friend, Sariah, outside your home. Her eyes sparkle with anticipation, mirroring your own excitement. "Ready for the adventure?" she asks, holding up her own jar, its glass faintly humming with enchantment.

"Always," you reply with a grin, holding up your jar in response.

Together with your two other friends, Taryn and Elara, who join you, bubbling with laughter and playful banter, you make your way to the edge of Meadowfen. The elders have already gathered, standing in a semi-circle, their faces illuminated by the soft glow of lanterns. They welcome you and the other young participants with nods of encouragement, reminding everyone of the race's spirit: to follow, to explore, but most importantly, to respect the fireflies and the secrets of the night.

As the final rays of the sun fade, a hush falls over the crowd. The elders begin the chant, old words that speak of harmony and adventure, and one by one, the jars in your hands begin to glow softly, ready to catch the magical fireflies. And then, as if on cue, the night comes alive with a thousand tiny lights. The Starlight Race has begun.

You and your friends dash into the fields, laughter filling the air as you chase the elusive fireflies. Sariah is quick, her movements swift and graceful, darting between beams of moonlight that break through the canopy. Finn, with his keen eyes, spots clusters of fireflies hidden away, leading you to secret gatherings of light. Elara, ever the strategist, suggests patterns and paths to follow, her mind always thinking a step ahead.

The fireflies lead you deeper into the enchanted woods than you've ever been. Here, the trees whisper ancient secrets, and the moon casts a silver sheen over everything, making the ordinary look extraordinary. You feel as if you're part of something much larger, a story woven with threads of light and shadow.

Wander deeper into the forest. (Go to page 7)

Finish the race with Sariah. (Go to page 10)

Ignore Sariah's calls and enter the Enchanted Forest.

As the sun began to set, casting long shadows through the Enchanted Forest of Eldoria, excitement bubbled within you. Today, you ventured further into the forest than ever before. With a backpack filled with snacks and a sturdy walking stick, you felt prepared for anything.

The trees seemed to whisper encouragement as you walked, their leaves rustling softly. Suddenly, you spotted flickers of light dancing in the underbrush just off the path. Driven by curiosity, you stepped off the path to follow the lights. They darted about playfully, leading you deeper into the woods.

You chased the lights over babbling brooks and under ancient trees, laughing as they always stayed just out of reach. But when the last light disappeared behind a large tree, you

realized you were lost. The friendly whispers of the trees now seemed distant, and the path was nowhere in sight.

Panic set in as you tried to retrace your steps, but everything looked the same. The underbrush seemed to hide watching shadows, and every rustle made your heart jump. Your adventure had turned into a scary quest to find your way home.

As darkness fell, the forest transformed into a maze of shadows and noises, intensifying your fear. "I shouldn't have wandered off," you thought, regretting your decision. Remembering advice from your best friend Sariah, you found a clear spot, sat down, and hoped for rescue, recalling her words: "If you ever find yourself lost, stay put. Help will come."

Wait until someone finds you. (Go to page 12)

Try to find your own way out. (Go to page 22)

Wander deeper into the forest.

Laughter and the sounds of other children fill the air, creating a melody of joy and excitement. "Let's see who can catch the most," Sariah challenges with a grin, her eyes shining with the thrill of the adventure.

You nod, feeling the rush of excitement. "You're on!" you exclaim, racing after the flickering lights that dance just beyond your reach. The fireflies lead you further into the Enchanted Forest of Eldoria, their lights weaving a path of enchantment through the trees. You are so focused on following them, marveling at how they seemed to tease and beckon you deeper, that you don't notice Sariah is no longer by your side.

The realization hits you suddenly. The laughter and voices of the other children have faded away, leaving only the whispers of the forest and the soft glow of fireflies. You stop, looking around, trying to spot Sariah's familiar figure or hear her voice calling out to you. But there is nothing. Just the dense trees and the quiet.

Panic flutters in your chest like a trapped bird. "Sariah?" you call out, your voice sounding small and alone among the towering trees. No answer comes except the echo of your own voice off the trees. You try to retrace your steps, hoping to find your way back to the meadow, to Sariah, and to safety. But the forest seems to shift around you, paths tangling and untangling in ways that make no sense.

The adventure that had filled you with excitement now twists into fear. The once-friendly flicker of the fireflies feel like distant stars, out of reach and offering no guidance. The darkness of the forest closes in, and the sounds of the night seem to whisper of mysteries and secrets you are too scared to understand.

You huddle under a large tree, hugging your knees close. "I just want to go home," you whisper, the thrill of the race forgotten. The realization of being truly lost in the Enchanted Forest of Eldoria, a place of wonders but also of dangers, weighs

heavily on your heart.

But even in the depths of your fear, the forest seemes to sense your distress. The aggressive flutter of wings and the eerie glow begin to soften, as if the forest and its creatures are trying to comfort you. The once teasing lights of the fireflies begin to gather, forming a glowing circle around you, their light pushing back the darkness and the fear.

In that moment, you realized that the forest, for all its mysteries, is trying to guide you back to safety. Drawing a deep breath, you stand up, the light from the fireflies casting a reassuring glow on the path ahead. "I'm not alone," you say to yourself, the fear begins to ebb as you think about returning to the warmth and safety of Meadowfen, guided by the gentle light of your newfound friends.

Doubt tickles the back of your mind. What if these fireflies are not leading you home? You remember one of the elders once telling you that if you were ever lost in the forest, you should wait where you are for someone to find you. You wonder if maybe that would be the wiser choice.

Wait until someone finds you. (Go to page 12)

Follow the fireflies. (Go to page 15)

Finish the race with Sariah

After what feels like both a moment and a lifetime, you find yourselves in a clearing you've never seen before, bathed in the light of countless fireflies. It's a hidden part of the forest, alive with magic, where the fireflies dance in mesmerizing patterns.

Sariah turns to you, her jar filled with the gentle light of the fireflies, her face alight with wonder. "I think we've found it," she whispers, "the heart of the Starlight Race."

Together, you release the fireflies, watching as they rise into the night sky, their lights merging with the stars above. In this moment, under the canopy of the Enchanted Forest and the vast universe beyond, you feel a profound connection to the world around you, to your friends, and to the adventure that awaits.

As you make your way back to Meadowfen, guided by the stars and the soft luminescence of your jars, now dim, you realize that the race was never just about catching fireflies. It was about the journey, the laughter shared, the mysteries embraced, and the magic that lives in the heart of every adventure.

When you finally arrive back in Meadowfen, the quiet village seems almost too normal after the enchanting race you just had. The warm glow of the fireflies' light still lingers in your memory, their gentle hum echoing in your mind. Sariah walks beside you, her eyes reflecting the same sense of longing for the extraordinary.

As you bid farewell to Sariah and the other racers, a bittersweet feeling settles within you. The Starlight Race may be over for this year, but its magic will forever remain etched in your heart. You watch as Sariah disappears around a bend, heading back to her own home.

Returning to your humble cottage, you can't help but feel disappointed by your ordinary, everyday life. The ticking of the clock on the mantel and the crackling of the fireplace seem dull compared to the vibrant world you just experienced. You sigh as you open the door and smell the sweet aroma of your mother's fresh bustle berry pie.

Reluctantly, you put aside the thoughts of adventure for another year, knowing that true adventure will have to wait until you grow up.

The End

Wait until someone finds you.

You're sitting quietly on a mossy log in the Enchanted Forest of Eldoria, your immediate area lit by the glowing fireflies. At first, the adventure was thrilling, and you chased after the flickering lights with all the excitement in your heart. But now, you're not so sure. You wandered too far, following those tricky lights, and suddenly, you can't find your way back. You don't recognize anything around you, and everything feels too quiet.

You decide to stay put, thinking it's the best way for someone to find you. "They'll notice I'm gone soon," you tell yourself, trying to stay hopeful. But as the minutes tick by, your hope starts to fade, and the forest seems to grow darker and bigger. The shadows stretch out like long fingers, the breeze through the trees seems to whisper as if telling sad tales of others who lost their way.

You shiver, hugging your knees tighter, wishing more than anything to be back in your cozy bed in Meadowfen. As the night wears on, you begin to feel a sense of unease creeping over you. The once comforting sounds of the forest now seem to hold a more sinister tone. Every rustle of leaves or hoot of an owl makes you jump, and the darkness feels like it's closing in on you.

You huddle closer to the log, trying to find comfort in its solid presence. But as the hours pass by and still no one comes to find you, your fears grow stronger. What if no one does come? What if you're lost in this enchanted forest forever? Your mind starts to conjure up all sorts of scary scenarios – monsters lurking in the shadows, witches casting spells, and other creatures waiting to trap unsuspecting wanderers like yourself.

Just when you're about to give up, convinced that adventures are way scarier than you ever imagined, you hear something. At first, it's faint, but then it grows clearer – voices calling your name.

"Over here!" you shout as loudly as you can, your voice breaking through the silence of the forest.

The lights of torches bob through the trees, getting closer and closer. And then, finally, familiar faces emerge from the darkness. It's your friends and some of the elders from Meadowfen, their faces full of relief and concern.

"We found you!" they exclaim, rushing over to make sure you're okay.

As they lead you back home, wrapped in a warm blanket someone thought to bring, you feel a mix of emotions. Relief washes over you at the sight of Meadowfen's twinkling lights, but there's also a bit of disappointment.

Adventures seemed so exciting in stories, but you hadn't expected to feel so scared and alone.

Back in your own bed, with the adventure behind you, you think about the day. You're incredibly grateful for your friends and the community that came to find you. Maybe adventures can be exciting, but for now, you decide, they're also pretty nice when they're over. And maybe, just maybe, some adventures can wait until you're a little older.

The End

Follow the fireflies.

You're tiptoeing through the Enchanted Forest of Eldoria, your eyes wide with wonder. The night is alive with magic, and in front of you, a cluster of fireflies glows brightly, leading you deeper into the forest. You can't help but follow them; their light is too inviting, too full of promise. They dance through the air, and you skip after them, your heart beating with the thrill of discovery.

Suddenly, the fireflies stop. They swirl in the air, forming a circle around something standing in the middle of a small clearing. You step closer, curious, and see it's an old stone pillar, covered in moss and vines. Beside the pillar lies a skeleton, its bony fingers clutching a rusty sword in one hand and a faded note in the other. The sight sends a shiver down your spine, but the mystery of it all pulls you closer.

You turn your attention to the pillar. The stone pillar is old and weathered, covered in layers of green moss and winding vines. It stands tall and proud in the center of the clearing, the fireflies forming a glowing halo around some carvings on the stone that seem to shift in the faint light, almost as if they are alive. The air in the clearing smells fresh and earthy, with a hint of moisture and decay from the surrounding forest. As you step closer to the pillar, you catch a whiff of musty stone and wet moss, mingling with the sweet scent of the fireflies. The fireflies seem to twinkle brighter as if urging you to take a closer look.

You glance at the skeleton, feeling a mix of sadness and determination. The skeleton is laid out on the ground, its bones, turned white with time, is a stark contrast against the dark forest floor. Its bony fingers are wrapped tightly around an old sword and a crumpled piece of parchment, both seeming out of place in the peaceful clearing. The parchment in its hand might hold some useful information. The sword might come in handy too.

Investigate the pillar. (Go to page 17)

Investigate the skeleton. (Go to page 20)

Investigate the pillar.

You step closer, curious, and see it's an old stone pillar, covered in moss and vines. Beside the pillar lies a skeleton, its bony fingers clutching a rusty sword in one hand and a faded note in the other. The sight sends a shiver down your spine, but the mystery of it all pulls you closer.

You turn your attention to the pillar, where words are etched into the stone. It's a poem, cryptic and ancient, and you read it out loud, your voice a whisper in the silent forest:

In the heart where shadows dwell,
Lies a secret none can tell.
Seek the crystal, pure and bright,
Hidden far from mortal sight.

Only those whose hearts are true,
Can claim the wish that they pursue.
Beware, for darkness cloaks the day,
Where the Crystal of Destiny lay.

Your eyes grow wide as you realize what you've found. The poem speaks of the Crystal of Destiny, a powerful artifact hidden somewhere in this very forest! The fireflies seem to twinkle brighter, as if urging you to solve the riddle and find the crystal.

As you stand before the old stone pillar, the words of the poem echo in your mind, sending a ripple of excitement through you. The Crystal of Destiny, a name that feels as magical as the forest around you, is hidden somewhere here, waiting to be found. You look around, half-expecting the forest to reveal its secrets right then and there, but the Enchanted Forest of Eldoria remains silent, its mysteries tightly held.

The fireflies dance around you, their light casting playful shadows on the ground. It's as if they're inviting you to think, to ponder the riddle before you. "In the heart where shadows dwell," you repeat softly, looking into the dense parts of the forest where the sun's rays hardly touch. Could the crystal be hidden in the darkest part of the forest, where shadows weave through the trees like threads of night?

"Seek the crystal, pure and bright," the next line guides you. Your mind races with possibilities. Maybe it's not just about finding a place where it's physically dark. Perhaps it's about finding a place filled with light, where the crystal's purity and brightness could hide in plain sight, like a star hidden by the sun's glare.

You glance at the skeleton beside the pillar, wondering if they, too, pondered these very thoughts. With a determined breath, you decide it's up to you to solve the riddle and uncover the whereabouts of the Crystal of Destiny.

Two possible interpretations of the poem's clues swirl in your mind, each leading you in a different direction:

Perhaps the poem is guiding you to venture deeper into the forest, into a place where the shadows are thickest, and the light barely penetrates. This could be the heart where shadows dwell, a place of mystery and danger, but also where the crystal's light could be hiding, waiting for someone brave enough to seek it out.

On the other hand, the crystal might be hidden somewhere that represents the "pure and bright" part of the poem. This could mean a clearing or a glade within the forest where sunlight shines the brightest, maybe there's a lake or waterfall, a place of purity and light that could conceal the crystal in its brilliance.

Look for the darkest part. (Go to page 26)

Look for the brightest part. (Go to page 29)

Investigate the skeleton. (Go to page 20)

Investigate the skeleton.

As you stand before the old stone pillar, your gaze slowly drifts back to the skeleton beside it. The sight of it, still and silent, sends a shiver down your spine, but your curiosity is stronger than your fear. You inch closer, compelled to learn more about this mysterious figure who once stood before this same pillar, just like you.

In one of the skeleton's hands, you notice a sword. Despite its age, the blade isn't rusted. It gleams under the light of the fireflies, as if some magic protects it from the passage of time. The sword looks strong and sturdy, capable of defending against unknown dangers that might lurk within the forest. Around the skeleton's waist, a leather scabbard is still fastened, its surface worn but intact.

The other hand clutches a crumpled-up piece of parchment. Age has yellowed its edges, and the writing that covers its surface is a

mystery waiting to be uncovered. You can see the ink has faded but not disappeared, words written by someone determined to leave a message behind. To read it, you'll have to carefully pull the parchment from the skeleton's grip.

You stand there in the silence of the forest, pondering your next move. The sword and the note each hold their own allure, their own secrets.

Taking the sword could offer you protection, a tangible link to the past and this unknown adventurer's quest. It feels like a piece of history, a tool that could help you navigate the dangers of the Enchanted Forest.

On the other hand, taking a closer look at the note could reveal valuable clues or wisdom left by the adventurer. It might hold the key to understanding more about the what lies ahead. The words on that parchment could be the very insight you need to guide your journey through the forest.

Faced with these options, you realize that each choice could significantly impact your adventure:

Investigate the pillar. (Go to page 17)

Take the sword. (Go to page 107)

Take a closer look at the note. (Go to page 109)

Try to find your own way out.

The forest around you grows darker, and the coolness of the evening begins to seep through your clothes. You wrap your arms around yourself, trying to keep warm, your heart thumping loudly in your chest. You wish more than anything that you could find your way back to the warmth and safety of home.

Then, just as you're starting to feel really scared, you notice something in the distance. It's a thin wisp of smoke, light-colored against the darkening sky, rising as if from a chimney. "Could it be?" you wonder, hope reigniting within you. Someone must be out there, maybe a cabin or a safe place where you can find help.

You stand up, brushing the leaves off your clothes, and start moving toward the smoke. Your walking stick feels reassuring in your hand as you navigate through the underbrush, which no longer seems as menacing now that you have a direction to follow. The forest, with all its mystery and whispers, becomes a bit friendlier again, encouraging you with every step.

As you make your way closer, the smoke becomes more visible, a sure sign of a fire and, hopefully, people. You quicken your pace, excitement mixed with a bit of nervousness. "What if they're not friendly?" a small voice in your head asks. But you push the thought away, focusing on the hope of finding help.

After a few minutes, you come upon a small clearing. There, right in front of you, is a cozy-looking cottage with light shining through its windows and smoke curling up from the chimney. You pause at the edge of the clearing, taking in the sight before you. The cottage is simple but charming, with a thatched roof and a small garden blooming with colorful flowers.

As you take a few hesitant steps forward, you notice that there is no path leading up to the cottage. It's as if it has appeared out of thin air. At the far edge of the clearing is a clearly defined path. There are several fireflies flitting around the mouth of the path. Every now and then as you watch, one of the fireflies leaves the group and moves closer to you before flitting back. It seems as if they are trying to lure you away from the cottage and down the path.

Approach the mysterious cottage. (Go to page 24)

Follow the fireflies. (Go to page 15)

Approach the mysterious cottage.

As you knock on the front door of the cottage, your heart beats a rapid rhythm, echoing the nervousness fluttering inside you. The door swings open with a groan, revealing an old man whose presence seems as rugged as the forest itself. His hair is a wild mane of gray, each strand rebelling against any sense of order, and his face is etched with lines that speak of years spent under the sun and wind of the Enchanted Forest. His eyes, sharp and scrutinizing, bore into you with an intensity that makes you momentarily uneasy.

"What do you want?" His voice is gruff, like the bark of the old trees surrounding his home, and it carries an edge of impatience. Despite this, there's a flicker of curiosity in his gaze, suggesting that your presence isn't entirely unwelcome.

"I... I got lost," you stammer, the words barely a whisper against the vastness of the forest's silence.

"Lost, huh?" he replies, his tone softening ever so slightly, but still laced with a skepticism that makes you doubt his intentions. "Many get lost in these woods. Few find their way to my door. What makes you different?"

You're not sure how to answer, feeling the weight of his gaze assessing you. Before you can muster a reply, he sighs heavily, as if the decision is being pulled from him against his better judgment.

"Fine. You can come in. But don't think this means I'm here to coddle you," he grumbles, stepping aside to allow you entry into the cottage. His demeanor is prickly, like a thorn-bush, yet the offer of refuge is there, hidden beneath the brambles of his gruff exterior.

As you cross the threshold, you notice the old man's eye flicker again, that unsettling quirk that sends a ripple of doubt through your mind. It's brief, but it's there—a hint of something unreadable, a shadow passing over his features. It leaves you questioning, wondering about the stories hidden behind those eyes.

The cottage is warm, a stark contrast to the chill of the evening air. The scent of herbs hangs in the space, mingling with the aroma of a recently doused fire. It's inviting, yet the old man's abrupt manner and that odd flicker in his eye have sown a seed of doubt. Can you trust him, or is it safer to keep your guard up?

As you stand there, two options present themselves, each path diverging from this moment of uncertainty:

Accept his invitation and stay. (Go to page 31)

Politely decline and leave. (Go to page 35)

Look for the darkest part of the forest.

Eager to uncover the secrets of the Enchanted Forest of Eldoria and find the Crystal of Destiny, you decide to follow the clue from the poem. You're looking for "the heart where shadows dwell," convinced that this dark, mysterious place could be where the crystal is hidden. With determination in your heart, you venture deeper into the forest, away from the familiar paths and into the unknown.

As you walk, the ground beneath your feet becomes soft and spongy, squishing slightly with each step you take. The once proud and lofty canopy of trees now surrenders to a chaotic and twisted realm of foliage, a thicket of branches and vines that seem to reach out and ensnare any who dare to pass through. The vines hang like a veil, obscuring the path and forcing you to wrestle your way through, testing your determination and bravery, the rustling of leaves and the creaking of branches surround you as you make your way through. The musty, earthy scent of the forest is intensified here, as though the very heart of the forest has its own unique perfume. The dampness and decay mingle with the sweet, pungent fragrance of wildflowers. It's as if the forest itself is trying to slow you down, to make you think twice about continuing.

Eventually, you reach a crossroads where the path you've been following splits into two very different directions. To your left, there's a rough trail that leads into a misty swamp. The air is thick with fog, and you can just make out the shape of twisted trees rising from the water. The path looks uncertain and treacherous, but the swamp's mysterious allure tugs at your curiosity.

On your right, there's a dark cave. The mouth of the cave yawns wide, its rocky walls slick with moisture. The darkness within swallows any light that touches it, making it impossible to see what lies ahead. It stands like a mouth ready to swallow you whole. The air around the cave is musty and damp, the scent of wet earth and decaying leaves filling your nostrils. But there's also a faint aroma of something sweet, almost enticing, mixed in with the musty smell. It's a combination that both repels and draws you closer.

As you approach the cave, the air grows colder and more damp, sending a shiver down your spine. The rough walls feel jagged and uneven under your fingertips, almost as if they are alive. Peering in, it's impossible to see what lies inside from where you're standing. Like a forbidden temptation, equal parts thrill and terror, daring you to step into the unknown and discover what lurked within its depths.

Faced with these two choices, you realize that each offers a very different journey into the unknown. Each option leads deeper into the mysteries of the Enchanted Forest of Eldoria. Will you brave the uncertain paths of the swamp, or will you seek out the secrets hidden in the darkness of the cave?

Go through the misty swamp. (Go to page 58)

Enter the dark cave. (Go to page 38)

Look for the brightest part of the forest.

With the poem's words echoing in your mind, you decide to seek out the "pure and bright" part of the forest, convinced that the Crystal of Destiny must be hidden in a place filled with light. Your heart beats with excitement and hope as you begin your search, looking for any sign of brilliance that could lead you to the crystal.

As you wander through the forest, the dense canopy above seems to part, allowing more sunlight to filter through the leaves. The air feels warmer here, and the sounds of the forest seem to sing a welcoming tune. Then, you see it—a glimmer of light through the trees, not just the green of the leaves but something more, something that calls to you.

You find yourself battling through the underbrush, where thick green ferns stretch up like miniature barriers, and the ground is tangled with vines that seem to grab at your feet. Colorful wildflowers peek out from between the greenery, but their beauty is almost lost in the struggle as you push and weave your way through. Each step forward requires effort, as if the forest itself is testing your determination to explore its hidden depths. The scent of the forest is alive, mixed with the freshness of flowing water. As you move closer to the source of the light, the sound of cascading water grows louder, guiding your steps.

Finally, you step into a clearing, and the sight takes your breath away. In front of you lies a small pond, its surface shimmering under the sun. The pond is fed by a waterfall, a graceful ribbon of water that catches the light, creating a mist that glows with rainbow hues. The sun, high in the sky, bathes the clearing in a warm, golden light, making the mist sparkle like tiny stars.

It's a place of undeniable beauty and peace, exactly the kind of "pure and bright" location mentioned in the poem. As you step closer to the pond, you wonder if the Crystal of Destiny could really be hidden in such an enchanting spot.

Explore the waterfall. (Go to page 45)

Search the mist-shrouded pond. (Go to page 47)

Accept his invitation and stay.

Deciding to trust the gruff old man, you step into his cottage, enveloped by the warm glow of the fireplace. The interior is cozy, filled with the aroma of something delicious cooking. The old man motions for you to sit at a small wooden table before turning back to tend to a pot simmering over the fire. Soon, he places a bowl of steaming stew in front of you, its savory scent making your stomach growl in appreciation.

As you savor the warmth of the stew, the old man leans back in his chair, the fire casting shadows that dance across the walls of the cottage. He seems to relax slightly, though his eyes never quite lose their guarded edge.

"I was an adventurer once, much like you," he starts, stirring his own stew absentmindedly. "Came to this forest in search of—something mystical. Something not meant for the eyes of the greedy. I was younger then, full of dreams and ambitions," he continues, his voice taking on a reflective quality. "The forest was different in those days, less—less cautious of strangers. Or perhaps it was just as wary, but I was too brash to notice."

He chuckles, a low sound that seems to rumble from deep within him. "I spent years searching for it. The Heart of the Forest. It wasn't just the power I was after, you understand. It was the challenge, the adventure. The Heart was said to be hidden in the deepest part of Eldoria, guarded by the very essence of the forest itself."

As he takes a moment to savor his stew, his gaze shifts to you once more. "I faced countless trials," he begins,

his voice tinged with sadness. "But the worst ones were when we— I had to face the illusions that tested my sanity. But the true struggle was the deafening silence and crushing loneliness. But now... nature is my only companion." His voice trembled with a hint of sadness, as if he were remembering something lost along the way.

The old man's gaze drifts to the flames. "When I finally found the Heart, it was not in a grand temple or guarded by some fearsome beast. It was nestled within the roots of the oldest tree in the forest, as if it had simply been waiting for someone worthy to come along."

He leans forward, his voice lowering. "But power brings temptation. I knew then that it couldn't be allowed to fall into the wrong hands. So, I stayed, became its guardian. All these year, protecting the heart, I learned something important."

He looks you straight in the eye, the flicker of suspicion replaced for a moment by earnestness. "The true power of the Heart, or any power for that matter, isn't in how you can change the world around you. It's in how you let it change you, for better or worse. Remember that. And remember, the forest watches, listens. Treat it with respect, and it will guide you. Disrespect its gifts, and you'll find nothing but shadows and misfortune."

The old man sits back, his piece said, leaving you to think about his words. In his tale, and his advice, lies a deeper understanding of the Enchanted Forest of Eldoria and perhaps the key to navigating its mysteries.

As sit thinking about the old man's words, you notice a shift in his demeanor. The initial warmth in his eyes cools, replaced by a glint of suspicion. It's as if by sharing his secret, he's suddenly remembered you're a stranger, potentially a threat to the treasure he's dedicated his life to protecting.

His jaw tenses, and the lines on his weathered face deepen as he studies you intently. The crackling fire casts eerie shadows that flicker across the small room, enhancing the tense atmosphere. The warmth that once enveloped the cozy cottage seems to retreat, leaving a chill in its wake.

"You," he says slowly, his voice now tinged with suspicion, "you didn't just stumble upon this place by chance, did you? You were sent to take the Heart of the Forest from me! That's why you're asking all these questions, prying into things you know nothing about!" His eyes narrow accusingly, searching for any sign of deception in your expression.

The old man's hands grip the edges of the wooden table, his knuckles white with tension. His once kind gaze now holds a sharp edge, and a protective air surrounds him like a cloak. His protective instincts flare up like a well-guarded flame, wary of any threat to the precious Heart of the Forest nestled within the roots of Eldoria.

His hand unconsciously drifts towards a hidden pocket within his cloak, where a glimmer of something precious catches the firelight. The bowl of stew before you suddenly feels heavy as his defensive stance puts

The atmosphere in the cottage changes, becoming charged with an unspoken question: Do you pose a danger to the old man's secret?

Reassure him of your intentions. (Go to page 40)

Try to take the Heart of the Forest. (Go to page 43)

Politely decline and leave.

The unease stirred by the flicker in his eye, that momentary shift in expression, is enough to make you reconsider. Trusting your instincts has always served you well. The forest may hold dangers, but your intuition might just be the key to navigating them safely.

With a polite, but muffled word, you back out of the cabin and into the clearing. At the far edge of the clearing is a clearly defined path. The fireflies are still flitting around the mouth of the path. Every now and then as you watch, one of the fireflies leaves the group and moves closer to you before flitting back. It seems as if they are trying to lure you away from the cottage and down the path.

Follow the fireflies. (Go to page 15)

Go back the way you came. (Go to page 36)

Go back the way you came.

After leaving the old man's cottage, feeling a mix of relief and unease, you decide to try and find your way back the way you came. The night has fully settled over the Enchanted Forest of Eldoria now, and without the fireflies' gentle glow to guide you, the path is shrouded in darkness. The trees loom large and mysterious, their branches whispering secrets you can no longer understand.

You walk cautiously at first, trying to remember landmarks or signs that might lead you back to familiar ground. But in the darkness, everything looks different, and the comforting signs of the path you followed into the forest have disappeared. The only sound is the crunch of leaves underfoot and the occasional distant call of a night creature.

As you press on, hoping against hope that you'll somehow find your way, the ground suddenly gives way beneath you. There's no time to react, no time to grab onto anything. You fall, tumbling into a ravine hidden by the shadows of the night. Pain shoots through your leg as you land with a thud at the bottom of the ravine. The sharp, undeniable pain tells you instantly that your leg is broken.

Lying there, the reality of your situation sinks in. You were warned about the dangers of the Enchanted Forest, especially at night, but the thrill of adventure pushed those warnings to the back of your mind. Now, injured and alone, you realize how foolish it was to wander the dark forest.

With no way to travel because of your broken leg, you start calling for help, hoping that someone, anyone, might hear you. But as the hours pass, your voice grows hoarse, and the forest remains silent, indifferent to your plight.

You can't help but think about the old man in the cottage. Maybe he knew this would happen. Maybe that's why he looked at you with such intensity, as if trying to warn you of the dangers that lay ahead. But it's too late for regrets now. All you can do is wait and hope for a miracle.

As the night wears on, you realize the Enchanted Forest of Eldoria might claim you as another of its young victims, lost to the allure of its mysteries and the darkness of its depths. The forest, for all its beauty during the day, becomes a different place at night—one that's not so forgiving of mistakes.

Lying there, you make a promise to yourself. If you make it out, you'll never underestimate the forest again, and you'll make sure others know to respect its power, especially when the sun goes down. But for now, all you can do is wait, listen to the forest's whispers, and hope for dawn.

Enter the dark cave.

Deciding to brave the darkness, hoping you interpreted the poem on the pillar correctly, you step into the mouth of the cave. A chill envelops you as the light from outside begins to fade. The cave swallows you into its shadows, and you can't help but feel a thrill mixed with a little bit of fear. You stretch your left hand out to touch the cave wall, letting it guide you as you move forward. As you run your hand along the wall, you can hear the pitter-patter of water droplets hitting the ground, a soothing symphony amidst the oppressive silence of the cave. The wall is smooth to the touch, and the dampness clings to your fingers, making them slightly sticky. The dampness leaving a slight chill on your fingers.

As you cautiously make your way through the dimly lit tunnel, a strange sound catches your attention. It's faint at first, barely audible over the echoing drip of water droplets. But as you continue forward, it grows louder and more distinct. It's a squelching noise, like wet shoes trudging across a muddy floor. You can feel your heartbeat quicken as you realize something is approaching from your right, and it's getting closer with each passing moment. Fear grips you as the sound intensifies and you brace yourself for whatever is about to emerge from the shadows. You freeze, listening closely. The sound is strange, not scary, but definitely not something you're used to hearing. Then, you notice a soft glow coming from the direction of the noise. It's a gentle, pulsing light, like the beat of a heart, lighting up the darkness around you.

Curiosity overcomes your initial fear, and you cautiously move towards the light. As you get closer, the source of the glow becomes clear—a magical creature unlike anything you've seen before. It's small and round, with a body that looks like it's made of jelly. The creature squelches along the cave floor, leaving a trail of soft light behind it. Its skin is translucent, and inside, you can see a gentle light glowing, lighting up the cave with each pulse.

This creature seems to be at home in the pitch-black cave, its bioluminescence a beacon in the darkness. Watching it move, you realize that this encounter could mean two different things for your adventure:

Follow the glowing creature. (Go to page 50)

Search the cave on your own. (Go to page 48)

Reassure him of your intentions.

In the warmth of the old man's cottage, with the fire crackling softly in the background, you find the courage to speak up. Your voice is steady, sincere as you assure him of your intentions. You explain that your journey into the forest was driven by curiosity and a deep respect for its mysteries, not a desire to claim the Heart of the Forest for yourself.

The old man listens, his suspicion slowly melting away as he hears the honesty in your words. A long moment passes, the only sounds are the pop and hiss of the fire and the gentle bubbling of the stew. Finally, he leans back, the tension easing from his shoulders as he offers a weary smile. "Forgive me," he says, his voice softer now, tinged with a hint of regret. "Years of solitude, guarding the Heart, it's made me wary of strangers."

He then shares a tale from his past, a time when he, too, was an adventurer driven by the thrill of the unknown. He speaks of his search for the Heart of the Forest, a quest that led him deep into Eldoria's ancient woods. When he finally discovered the Heart, nestled within the roots of the oldest tree, he was overcome with a fear unlike any he had faced before. The fear of losing the Heart to others consumed him, driving him to isolate himself from the world, to live as a hermit, guarding his treasure.

After finishing his story, the old man leads you through the forest to a clearing where a stone pillar stands, shrouded in moss and vines. The sight of it, especially the skeleton at its base, sends a chill through you. The air is heavy with the scent of earth and the faint glow of fireflies, lending an ethereal quality to the scene.

In the clearing, bathed in the soft glow of twilight, the old man's demeanor softens as he gazes at you with eyes that have seen many seasons pass within the forest's embrace. The air around you is filled with the whispers of ancient trees, and the occasional call of a distant bird breaks the silence, adding to the solemn atmosphere of the moment.

"Young traveler," he begins, his voice carrying the weight of wisdom and experience, "the path you've chosen is not for the faint of heart. The forest you seek to traverse is ancient and alive, filled with mysteries that have confounded many who've dared to unravel them."

He pauses, allowing the gravity of his words to sink in, then points towards the stone pillar standing solemnly in the clearing. Its surface is weathered, telling tales of time and the countless stories it has witnessed. "All great adventures begin with a choice," he says, his gaze fixed on the pillar. "The challenges you will face in this forest will demand more than strength and bravery. Wit, wisdom, and a keen sense of the world around you will be your true allies."

The old man steps closer to the pillar, his hand gently brushing against the moss and vines that cloak its surface. "This pillar," he continues, "is more than just stone and moss. It represents the crossroads of fate and free will, a reminder that every step forward is a choice made, a path taken."

He turns to you, a serious glint in his eyes. "The forest will test you, not just your courage, but the depth of your heart and the strength of your convictions. It will take more than sheer will to find what you seek. Remember, the true essence of any quest lies not in the destination, but in the journey itself and the choices you make along the way."

With a solemn nod towards the pillar, he imparts one final piece of advice: "Let this pillar be your first challenge. How you approach it, and the decisions you make here, will set the tone for your journey. Choose wisely, for every choice echoes in the heart of the forest."

Investigate the pillar. (Go to page 17)

Ask about the skeleton. (Go to page 105)

Try to take the Heart of the Forest.

As you listen to the old man's stories and advice, a plan begins to form in your mind. Despite his warnings and the wisdom he's shared, the allure of the Heart of the Forest is too strong. You nod and smile, pretending to agree with his views on power and respect for the forest, but inside, you're imagining how the Heart could change your own fate.

When the old man gets up to stoke the fire, you see your chance. With a quick glance around to ensure the Heart is still where he indicated earlier, you make your move. "I just want to see it," you say, trying to sound innocent. "To witness its beauty up close."

The old man's eyes narrow, sensing the shift in your intentions. "I've told you, the Heart isn't something to be toyed with," he warns, stepping in front of you, blocking your path.

Ignoring his words, you try to dart around him, reaching for the place where the Heart is hidden. But the old man is quicker than he looks, and with a swift motion, he uses the Heart to call upon the forest's protection.

Suddenly, the cottage feels alive. Branches and vines start creeping in through the windows and under the doors, twisting and turning, reaching for you. You dodge and weave, fighting off the persistent vines with all your might, determined to reach the old man and claim the Heart for yourself.

You corner him next to the fire, the light casting ominous shadows across his face. For a moment, fear flickers in his eyes, but then, with a deep, regretful sigh, he whispers a command to the Heart.

Vines burst forth from the floorboards, thick and unyielding, wrapping around your ankles and dragging you down. You struggle, trying to free yourself, but the vines are too strong. They pull you into the dirt floor of the cottage, burying you alive, the earth closing over your head.

The last thing you see is the old man standing above you, a look of sorrow mixed with disappointment on his face. "Betrayal," he says, his voice echoing in the closing darkness, "is the quickest path to ruin. The forest protects its own, and punishes those who would do it harm."

His words are the last thing you hear as the earth swallows you, a final, memorable warning about the consequences of greed and betrayal

The End

Explore the waterfall.

Walking closer to the waterfall, you can't help but be amazed. The water tumbles down like a shiny, liquid curtain, sparkling in the sunlight as if it's made of thousands of tiny diamonds. The sound of the water crashing into the pond below is loud, like nature's own music, filling the air around you with a refreshing mist that tickles your face and arms.

As you get closer, you notice that the water isn't just falling straight down; there's a space behind the waterfall, like a secret room hidden by the flowing water. Curiosity bubbling inside you like a geyser, you carefully make your way over slippery rocks and through the cool, misty air, moving closer to this hidden spot.

Reaching the waterfall, you find that the heavy veil of water hides a narrow passage. It's like stepping into another world—the noise of the waterfall becomes a dull roar behind you, and the air is cooler, filled with the scent of rain and earth. With a deep breath, filled with excitement and a touch of nerves, you climb through the space behind the waterfall.

To your surprise, you find yourself standing at the mouth of a dark cave. The light from outside barely reaches inside, making the cave's depths a mystery. It feels like you've discovered a secret, a place untouched and waiting to be explored.

Now, standing at the entrance of this dark cave behind the waterfall, you face a choice.

Enter the dark cave. (Go to page 38)

Search around the entrance. (Go to page 52)

Search the mist-shrouded pond.

You approach the mist-covered pond. The air feels magical, filled with tiny droplets that sparkle like rainbows in the sunlight. The waterfall is a constant, soothing, and powerful roar.

The mist swirls around your feet, making the ground beneath you seem dreamlike. You reach the pond's edge, where the water is calm and clear, reflecting the sky above. Peering into the depths, you search for a sign, a glimmer, anything indicating the crystal's presence.

Then, you see it—a faint glow beneath the water's surface, soft and elusive, like the first star at twilight. A thrill runs through you, a mix of excitement and disbelief. Could it really be the Crystal of Destiny?

The glow beckons you, urging you to reach out and claim the prize. Diving in would be a leap of faith, a testament to your bravery and determination. The cold water and unknown depths don't matter. You want the crystal, and you're willing to immerse yourself completely in the quest to retrieve it.

Dive in to get it. (Go to page 54)

Find something to fish it out with. (Go to page 56)

Search the cave on your own.

Guided by a sense of adventure and a trust in your own instincts, you make the decision not to follow the bioluminescent creature deeper into the cave. Instead, you turn your attention to the path it emerged from, a narrow, winding tunnel that promises its own secrets. The creature's passage has left a trail of bioluminescent slime on the walls and floor, casting a soft, blue glow that lights your way. It's like walking under a starlit sky, each step illuminated by the creature's eerie light.

As you venture further, the glow begins to fade, each footprint less luminous than the last, casting long shadows across the cave floor. The darkness grows, pressing in from all sides, a reminder of the unknown that lies ahead. But as you trudge on, a faint light appears in the distance. A glimmer of hope or just another cruel trick of the cave's unrelenting darkness? You dare not get your hopes up, but the light beckons you forward nonetheless.

With the light of the creature's slime dimming, you feel a sense of urgency and pick up your pace, freedom or trickery, you will need to find out soon. Drawn towards the hope of the light, you round another corner and the fresh breeze that whispers of open spaces brushes against your cheeks. The air, cool and inviting, fills your lungs, a stark contrast to the stagnant atmosphere of the cave's depths.

But as you approach, your heart sinks. Between you and the light, there's a pit, its depths lost in an impenetrable darkness. The edge is crumbling, the ground beneath your feet unsure.

Faced with this new obstacle, you realize you have two choices:

Find a way to cross the pit. (Go to page 74)

Search for another path. (Go to page 72)

Follow the glowing creature.

In the shadowed embrace of the cave, where darkness weaves its silent tales, you find yourself following the creature, a creature whose light promises guidance through the murky depths. Its body emits a soft, ethereal glow, a beacon in the consuming blackness that surrounds you. The creature moves swiftly, leaving behind a trail of bioluminescent slime that illuminates the path but only for fleeting moments before fading away.

Driven by a blend of curiosity and desperate hope, you hasten your steps, eager not to lose this living lantern in the twisting passages of the cave. The dank, stagnant air of the cave presses against your skin like a heavy blanket, weighing you down with each breath you take. The scent of earth and decay mingle in the confined space, filling your nose with a musty aroma that makes your stomach churn. As you follow the glowing creature deeper into the shadows, the air grows colder, sending shivers down your spine and raising goosebumps on your arms.

As you navigate the winding passages, the light from the creature becomes your world, a narrow tunnel of visibility in an ocean of dark. The thought of the Crystal of Destiny, possibly lying just ahead, quickens your pulse. Up ahead, around a bend in the cave's throat, a bright light beckons—a promise of escape, of reaching the end of your perilous journey. Your heart leaps at the thought, and with reckless abandon, you rush towards the light, anticipation fueling your steps.

The truth that awaits you is not the freedom you envisioned. Rounding the corner, you're not met with the open arms of the outside world but with the gaping maw of a monstrous version of the creature you've been following. It's a titan, dwarfing its smaller kin, its body a grotesque mass of glowing flesh and writhing tentacles.

One of its massive tentacles lashes out with terrifying speed, coiling around you with an inescapable grip. You struggle, but it's futile; the creature drags you towards its waiting mouth. A cavernous pit lined with rows of sharp, glistening teeth is the last thing you see before darkness claims you as the grotesque mouth of the creature closes around you.

The End

You stand at the base of a towering waterfall. The cascade of water is a curtain of shimmering droplets, casting a mist that clings to your skin and chills your bones. The ground beneath your feet is slick, the rocks coated with a treacherous layer of moisture that threatens to send you tumbling with every step you take.

As you edge closer to the waterfall, searching for any sign that might lead you to the Crystal of Destiny, your feet slip several times on the wet stones. Each slip sends your heart racing, a stark reminder of the peril that lies just a misstep away—the jagged rocks and churning water below, hungry for mistakes.

Lifting your gaze, you spy something intriguing carved into the rock face far above—a symbol

or message, perhaps a clue to the crystal's location. But reaching it poses a new challenge, as two distinct paths present themselves, each with its own dangers and promises.

To your left is a steep ascent. You will need to use all your strength and precision to climb the almost vertical surface. The rocks here offer some holds, but they are few and far between, and the risk of a fall is high. Yet, this path promises a more direct route to the carving, a test of your determination and physical prowess.

To your right, the path involves navigating closer to the waterfall itself, where the rocks are even more treacherous, slick with the constant spray of water. Halfway across, a thick vine hangs down, swaying gently in the mist, offering a way to bypass some of the climb. This route is no less dangerous, as the pounding water threatens to dislodge you, and trusting your weight to the vine requires a leap of faith in the forest's unpredictable nature.

Now, standing at the crossroads of decision, two paths lie before you:

Attempt the rock climb. (Go to page 67)

Brave the waterfall and use the vine. (Go to page 70)

Dive in to get it.

In the shadowed heart of the Enchanted Forest, where whispers of ancient magic lingered like fog, you stood at the edge of a dark, ominous pond. The chilling tales of those who had ventured into these woods and never returned echoed in your mind, a warning unheeded. Driven by a reckless desire for glory and the whispers of a hidden treasure, you cast aside caution and dived into the murky depths.

The water was cold, a biting chill that seeped into your bones, a harsh reminder of the forest's unforgiving nature. Surfacing, you gasped for air, the thrill of the hunt overshadowing the wisdom of restraint. Ignoring the ominous signs, you dove again, deeper this time, drawn to a shifting glow beneath the water.

As you approached, the light revealed itself not as the promised treasure but as a creature of the deep, its bioluminescence a lure for the unwary. Its beauty was mesmerizing, yet within its glow lay a predator, ancient and cunning. In your blind pursuit of glory, you had failed to see the truth that lay beneath the surface.

The creature struck, swift and relentless. Its embrace was inescapable, pulling you further into the abyss. In this moment of despair, the consequences of your choices became painfully clear. The forest, with all its enchanting allure, demanded respect—a respect you had forsaken in your arrogance.

As the darkness of the depths claimed you, a tragic realization washed over you. The quest for the Crystal of Destiny, driven by vanity rather than virtue, had been your undoing. The forest's secrets were not for the greedy heart, and your failure to heed its warnings had led you to this fate.

In the end, the Enchanted Forest reclaimed what was its, leaving behind a tale of caution for those who would follow. The moral etched in the very essence of the forest: that bravery without wisdom is folly, and the pursuit of power, without consideration for the consequences, leads only to downfall.

The End

Find something to fish it out with.

In the shadowy realm of the Enchanted Forest, where every leaf and stone holds a secret, you stand at the water's edge, wary of the unknown depths. The glow beneath the surface beckons, but you remember the tales of those who ventured too boldly and paid the price.

Despite the pull of the glow, a part of you hesitates to dive into the unknown waters. Instead, you search the area for a tool to aid your quest—a long stick that might reach the mysterious glow without requiring you to enter the water.

After a brief search among the twisted trees and underbrush, you find a stick, long and sturdy, seemingly waiting for you. With a deep breath, you extend the stick over the water, poking and prodding into the depths, hoping to coax the source of the glow closer to the shore.

For a moment, there's resistance, as if you've caught something. The glow at the bottom shifts, and your heart races with anticipation. But suddenly, the stick is yanked from your grasp with surprising force. Your eyes widen as the glow intensifies and begins to rise toward the surface, not slowly as a floating object might, but swiftly, with purpose.

Bursting from the water is a creature of nightmares and wonder—a bioluminescent being, its body pulsating with light. It's larger than you imagined, with tentacles that ripple and flail, each one lined with shimmering lights that illuminate the dark water around it. The creature's skin is translucent, revealing a network of glowing veins that pulse with an otherworldly energy. Its eyes, if it can be said to have eyes, are mere black spots on its head, focusing intently on you with a soulless intelligence that belies its monstrous form.

As you stand, frozen by the sight of this luminous sentinel of the depths, you realize that your quest for the crystal has awakened something ancient, something that the forest lulled to sleep with the mist-shrouded waterfall— kept hidden beneath the tranquil surface of the pond.

Now, this ancient creature had awakened and you stand in its black and soulless gaze.

Attempt to communicate. (Go to page 62)

Retreat and reconsider your approach. (Go to page 64)

Follow the trail through the misty swamp.

With a determined breath, you choose the trail through the misty swamp, believing it might hide the heart where shadows dwell and, with it, the Crystal of Destiny. The path before you is shrouded in fog, making the world around you appear like a scene from a dream. The mist curls around your ankles as you step forward, each movement sending small swirls dancing through the air.

Carefully, you hop from stone to stone, the only solid patches in a sea of murky water. Each jump brings a mix of thrill and relief, but as you progress, you notice the stones becoming scarcer until, finally, there are none left. With no other choice, you gather your courage and lower yourself into the cool, dark waters of the swamp.

The water is deeper than you expected, reaching up to your waist, making every step a struggle against the mud and water plants that tug at your legs. The silence of the swamp is heavy, broken only by the soft splashes of your movements. You push forward, determined to find what secrets the swamp might hold.

But then, something changes. You're so focused on finding a way through the water that you don't notice the ripples around you, gentle at first, then growing more pronounced, more purposeful. It's not until a shadow looms up from the murky depths that you realize you're not alone.

An alligator, its eyes just above the waterline, stares directly at you, its intent clear. Panic floods through you as the alligator moves closer, its powerful body cutting through the water with ease.

In this moment, frozen by fear and surprise, you understand the true dangers of the Enchanted Forest of Eldoria. The swamp, with all its mystery and beauty, is also a place of peril, home to creatures like the alligator, guardians of its secrets.

The alligator lunges towards you, its massive jaws gaping open to reveal row upon row of sharp, gleaming teeth. You try to back away, but the alligator is too fast. Its jaws snap shut around your leg. You scream in agony, the sound echoing through the silent swamp, mixing with the thrashing of the water and the alligator's triumphant hiss. You have time for one quick breath as the alligator pulls you under the murky water with terrifying force. Panic fills your chest as you struggle against the powerful predator, thrashing wildly in a futile attempt to break free.

The world around you blurs as the alligator drags you deeper into the dark depths of the swamp. You can feel its razor-sharp teeth piercing through your skin, sending waves of searing pain through your body. Bubbles escape from your mouth as you fight for air, your lungs burning with the need to breathe.

Your heartbeat thunders in your ears, a rapid drumbeat of fear and desperation. The cold embrace of the water threatens to swallow you whole, its icy tendrils wrapping around you like a suffocating shroud. Your vision starts to fade as darkness creeps in from the edges, a chilling realization dawning upon you.

You're not going to make it out of this alive.

The End

Attempt to communicate with the creature.

In the heart of the shadowed forest, where secrets whisper from every leaf and shadow, you find yourself face-to-face with the bioluminescent creature, its tentacles undulating gently in the dim light. Its form is both beautiful and terrifying, a being of the deep forest that seems as ancient as the trees themselves. With a deep breath, you muster your courage, raising your arms in a universal gesture of peace and calling out to the creature, your voice echoing softly in the cavernous space. "I mean no harm," you say, hoping to bridge the gap between your worlds with words.

The creature halts in its tracks, its lithe body poised and still, as if weighing your intentions. Its eyes, dark and bottomless, seem to draw you in with their unblinking stare. A tension you can feel hangs in the air, stretching out each passing second as both you and the creature hold your breaths. The once vibrant forest now falls silent, as if nature itself is holding its breath in anticipation of what will happen next. The usual chorus of life fades away, leaving only the eerie silence and the piercing gaze of the creature before you.

Standing there, vulnerable yet defiant, you lock eyes with the creature whose gaze feels like it could cut through steel. Your heart races and your muscles tense as you await its judgement, the air heavy with anticipation and the dripping of water from the creature's raised tentacles echoing through the silence. Each breath feels ragged and unsteady as the weight of the moment presses down on you.

In a sudden and unexpected attack, the creature's tentacles lash out with lightning speed. One of them wraps around you, its grip as unyielding as steel. The jolt of contact shatters any hope of understanding as you desperately struggle against the embrace. But the creature's strength is overpowering, each tentacle tightening like a vice around your body. You are at its mercy, helpless against its relentless hold.

Dragged towards the water, you feel the cold shock of the pond's surface against your skin, a chilling embrace that steals your breath away. The creature pulls you deeper, the light from above fading as you are drawn into the depths. The pressure on your chest is immense, a crushing force that squeezes tighter with every inch you descend.

In these final moments, as darkness encroaches and your lungs scream for air, the tragic folly of your choice becomes clear. The forest, with all its beauty and danger, requires more than good intentions or hopeful words. It demands respect, understanding, and, above all, wisdom in navigating its mysteries.

Your vision dims, the last bubbles of air escaping from your lips as you sink further into the abyss. The creature, a guardian of the forest's secrets, becomes the last thing you see, a reminder of the price paid for failing to heed the lessons of the forest. Your tale ends in the silent depths, a caution to those who come after, that the path to understanding the mysteries of the Enchanted Forest is fraught with dangers, both seen and unseen.

<u>The End</u>

Retreat and reconsider your approach.

You make the difficult decision to retreat. The creature's sudden emergence, its tentacles flailing, has shaken you. As you back away, heart pounding, you watch it thrash in the water, its glow illuminating the pond with haunting light.

You retreat to the forest's edge, where dense trees stand like silent guardians. From this safer distance, you see the creature trying to pull itself from the water, its tentacles reaching toward you.

The dark forest around you offers a chance to regroup. The creature's power is undeniable, but so is your determination to find the Crystal of Destiny. You must act quickly, choosing a path that won't lead to disaster.

Remembering the pillar's words hinting the crystal is where shadows dwell, you reconsider venturing into the darker parts of the forest. Yet, you still feel drawn to the light. Facing the creature is dangerous but could prove your bravery and secure the crystal.

Look for the darkest part of the forest. (Go to page 26)

Fight the creature. (Go to page 65)

Attempt to communicate. (Go to page 61)

Fight the creature.

The creature before you, a guardian of mysteries and a being of the deep forest, looms like a shadow come to life. Its tentacles, lit by an eerie bioluminescent glow, sway with a hypnotic rhythm, a silent challenge to your resolve.

Determined to prove your bravery and secure the crystal, you scan the forest floor for a weapon. Among the scattered leaves and the creeping vines, your gaze falls upon an old staff, its wood gnarled and covered in moss, entwined with vines that speak of years forgotten. Beside it lies a tattered cloak and an old pack, the remnants of an adventurer who once stood where you stand now. The pack, torn open, its contents long claimed by the forest, serves as a grim reminder of the dangers that lurk within these woods.

Grasping the staff, you feel its weight, a solid presence in your hands. The wood, though old, holds a strength born from the heart of the forest. With a resolve that hardens like the ancient trees around you, you face the creature, the staff your only ally in this dance of danger.

You swing the staff with all your might, the air whistling as it cuts through the space between you and the creature. The impact when the wood meets the creature's flesh sends a jarring vibration through your arms, a shock of resistance that speaks of the creature's power. But the victory is fleeting. With a speed that belies its size, the creature's tentacle wraps around the staff, its grip unyielding. With a flick of its massive limb, the staff is wrenched from your grasp and thrown aside, discarded like a broken twig.

The creature advances, its tentacles undulating with a menacing grace. You stand there, weaponless and exposed, the reality of your choice crashing down like the weight of the night.

Now, with the staff gone and the creature's intent clear, you face a new choice. Despite the loss of your weapon and the looming threat of the creature, a part of you refuses to back down. To continue fighting is to embrace the sliver of hope that courage and determination alone might turn the tide. This choice is a stand against the darkness, a defiance of the fear that seeks to claim you. Beside the waterfall, the dark maw of the cave whispers promises of refuge, a chance to flee from the creature and perhaps find another way. This choice is a retreat into the unknown, a hope that the shadows within will offer protection and a path to survival.

Escape into the cave. (Go to page 38)

Continue fighting the creature. (Go to page 82)

Attempt the rock climb.

You stand at the base of the steep rock face, the waterfall's mist enveloping you like a shroud. The path upward is daunting, a vertical dance of courage and caution. Each handhold and foothold is a choice, a question asked by the rock: "Do you have the will to climb?"

Your hands find the first few grips easily enough, the rock cold and unyielding beneath your fingers. But as you

ascend, the challenge grows. A handhold crumbles without warning, sending a shower of stones into the void below. Your heart races, a beat skipped in the symphony of your climb.

Then, a foot slips, finding nothing but air where solid rock should have been. For a terrifying moment, you dangle by one hand, the roar of the waterfall thundering in your ears, a reminder of the chasm waiting with open arms should you fall. With a desperate lunge, you regain your footing, your breath heavy with the taste of fear and mist.

The climb tests you, each move a conversation with gravity, each slip a lesson in humility. But with grit and resolve, you pull yourself over the final ledge and arrive at the carving, your body trembling from the exertion and adrenaline.

Before you, etched into the ancient stone, are the cryptic lines you sought, their meanings as elusive as the shadows that dance across them:

> *In the heart of darkness, truth resides,*
> *Where followers falter, the brave one strides.*
> *Leap into the unknown, for therein power lies,*
> *Only then will you claim the ultimate prize.*

The words resonate with a profound depth, echoing the trials of your journey. They speak of courage not just in facing physical challenges but in confronting the darkness within oneself and the world.

Now, as the mist from the waterfall cools your weary body, two paths unfold before you, guided by the wisdom of the ancient carving. The warning against being a follower stirs a cautious curiosity within you. Perhaps blindly entering the cave is not the only way to demonstrate bravery. Exploring the surrounding area, seeking alternative routes or secrets hidden in the light, could also lead to the ultimate prize. This choice is a leap of a different kind, a decision to trust in your path and the wisdom to know that strength comes in many forms.

Leap from the rock wall. (Go to page 79)

Seek another way. (Go to page 76)

Brave the waterfall's edge and use the vine.

As you stand before the roaring waterfall, its spray misting over you like a cold whisper, you set your eyes on the vine dangling tantalizingly close. It seems like the easier path, a shortcut to avoid the daunting climb. With determination, you begin to maneuver over the wet, slippery rocks, each step a calculated risk in the dance between bravery and recklessness.

The rocks are slick with moss, treacherous with hidden dangers. More than once, your foot slips, sending a jolt of fear through your heart. You bang your knee hard against a rock, pain shooting up your leg, a harsh reminder of the waterfall's unforgiving nature. You press on, driven by the sight of the vine just within reach, ignoring the throb in your knee.

Another step, another slip. This time, your shin scrapes against the jagged edge of a rock, the sharp pain a stark contrast to the cold numbness of the water. Yet, the sight of the vine, swaying gently in the waterfall's breath, beckons you closer, a siren call to weary travelers.

Finally, with aching limbs and a heart full of hope, you reach for the vine. You give it a cautious tug, testing its strength, trusting it to bear your weight. But the forest, with its ancient wisdom and hidden truths, has one more lesson to teach. The vine, weakened by time and the relentless caress of the waterfall, gives way under your grasp.

In an instant, you're falling backward, a gasp of surprise lost in the roar of the water. You crash onto the rocks below, the impact driving the air from your lungs. The waterfall, indifferent to your plight, pushes you under, its weight a cold, suffocating blanket.

Panic sets in as you struggle against the water's embrace, your lungs burning for air. Then, in the dim light filtered through the water, you see it—a bioluminescent tentacle, undulating with a life of its own. It lashes out, wrapping around you with an otherworldly strength, dragging you deeper into the abyss as darkness claims your vision.

The forest reveals its final truth to you: the path of least resistance, the easier way, often hides the greatest risks. The Enchanted Forest, with all its beauty and danger, demands respect—a respect you learned too late, as the darkness of the depths claims you.

The End

Search for another path around the pit.

Turning away from the perilous pit, you decide to trust your instincts and search for another path. The cave around you is pitch black, a darkness so complete it feels like a weight against your skin. You move cautiously, your hands stretched out before you, fingers brushing against the cold, damp walls of the cave. The sound of your own breathing is loud in the silence, each inhale and exhale a beacon as you navigate by sound and touch.

After what feels like an eternity of tense, slow progression, a soft glow appears around a corner. Your heart, which has been a steady drum of cautious beats, flutters with hope. Light means a way out, a chance to escape the oppressive darkness that has swallowed you whole. With a surge of relief fueling your steps, you move towards the glow, eager for the promise of escape, of freedom.

But as you round the bend, the hopeful light morphs into the harbinger of a grim reality. The cave opens up into a larger chamber, illuminated not by the exit you so desperately sought but by the bioluminescent glow of a creature, vast and horrifying. It's the same kind as the bioluminescent guide you encountered before, but monstrously larger, its body a grotesque display of glowing flesh and writhing tentacles that twist and coil with a life of their own.

Before you can react, one of the creature's massive tentacles lashes out. It wraps around you with a force that steals the breath from your lungs, pulling you inexorably towards its gaping maw. The mouth is a nightmare come to life, lined with rows of sharp teeth that gleam in the creature's own eerie light.

As you're dragged closer, the creature's mouth opening wide to consume you, the tragic truth of your situation becomes painfully clear. In seeking to avoid one danger, you've stumbled into something far worse. Your choice to search for another path, made in the hopes of finding safety, has led you instead to this moment of peril.

The last thing you see as darkness claims you is the grotesque mouth of the creature closing around you, a final vision that seals your fate. This tragic end serves as a stark lesson: that the path of caution is not without its risks, and that sometimes, the greatest dangers lie in the unexpected, waiting for those who wander in search of the light.

The End

Find a way to cross the pit.

Guided by a sliver of hope and the fading glow of the bioluminescent slime, you stand before the gaping pit, its depths shrouded in mystery and darkness. The edge crumbles underfoot, a precarious ledge at the brink of the unknown. Your heart beats a frantic rhythm, echoing the whisper of adventure and the chill of danger that fills the air.

With no stones or branches within reach to aid your crossing, desperation seizes you. The light on the other side, a beacon in the overwhelming darkness, seems to call out to you, a challenge to your courage and a test of your resolve.

You step back, the cave floor cool and uneven beneath your feet, every sense heightened as you prepare to make the leap. The air is heavy with anticipation, the silence of the cave broken only by the steady drip of water, a countdown to the moment of decision.

With a deep breath, you steel yourself and run towards the edge. Your footsteps echo in the cramped space, a rapid drumbeat that marks your charge towards destiny. The edge approaches, the pit yawning wide before you, an abyss that threatens to swallow you whole.

You leap, the ground disappearing beneath you as you soar through the air. Time slows, each second stretched into eternity. The far side of the pit looms ahead, an uncertain target in the dim light. Your heart races, a wild thing trapped within your chest, as the dark depths of the pit rush by beneath you.

The suspense is palpable, a tangible thing that wraps around you, squeezing tight with the uncertainty of your fate. Will the leap be enough? Will your feet find solid ground, or will the darkness claim you?

As you fly across the chasm, two possibilities flash through your mind, each a choice that could shape your landing and your fate. You could try to tuck your body into a roll as you hit the ground, hoping to absorb the impact with your momentum. It's a technique you've heard of, a way to lessen the chance of injury when falling from a height. This choice relies on your agility and the hope that the cave floor on the other side is forgiving enough to allow such a maneuver. Alternatively, you could brace yourself to land on your feet, knees bent to absorb the shock. It's a riskier option, dependent on your legs' strength and your ability to withstand the force of the landing.

Tuck and roll upon landing. (Go to page 90)

Brace for impact with your legs. (Go to page 92)

Seek another way.

Clinging to the cliff face, with the waterfall's roar filling your ears and mist soaking your skin, you pause to catch your breath. The rough rock texture digs into your fingers, a harsh reminder of the perilous ascent. Your arms tremble from the strain as you glance downward. The waterfall crashes against the rocks below, sending sprays of icy water into the air. A rainbow shimmers in the mist, sunlight filtering through the canopy. The deafening sound reverberates through your bones. The waterfall cascades behind you, its spray a chilling companion.
Gathering courage, your gaze drifts upward to a shadowed nook in the cliff—a depression hinting at secrets within the stone. It beckons, promising answers or a new path. Your eyes return to cryptic words carved into the rock. Among the script, the word "leap" captures your attention. Below, the pond's dark waters suggest a literal plunge into the mysteries beneath. Pressed against the cliff's cold, wet surface, two daring options unfold before you.

Continue the climb up. (Go to page 78)

Take the leap into the pond below. (Go to page 80)

Continue the climb towards the depression.

With a deep breath to steady your racing heart, you decide to continue your climb towards the shadowed nook in the cliff, the depression that promises secrets and perhaps even a path forward. Each movement is deliberate, a balance between caution and the need to reach the unseen. The waterfall's spray makes the rock slick beneath your fingers, a constant challenge as you inch your way upward.

Finally, when your shaking arms can't seem to take any more, your hand finds the edge of the depression. With a grunt of effort, you pull yourself up and over the lip, collapsing onto solid ground for the first time in what feels like an eternity. Your relief is palpable, a heavy sigh escaping your lips as you take a moment to rest.

As your breath returns to you, and your eyes adjust to the dim light, you notice that the depression isn't just a feature of the rock face but the entrance to a passage that leads deep into the heart of the cliff itself. The mouth of the cave yawns before you, an invitation to the dark unknown.

Curiosity wars with caution within you. This passage could be the key to unlocking the mysteries you seek, a hidden route to wonders untold. Yet, the darkness is intimidating, a stark reminder that not all paths lead to light. The cave could hold answers, or it could be a journey into depths from which there is no return.

Descend into the dark cavern. (Go to page 38)

Climb back down to solid ground. (Go to page 84)

Take the leap into the pond below.

Clinging to the rough, unforgiving face of the cliff, your fingers find precarious purchase on the small ledges and crevices that pockmark its surface. The mist from the waterfall shrouds you like a damp cloak with is a ghostly embrace, seeping into your pores and and sending shivers down your spine. Below, the pond awaits, its surface obscured by the veil of falling water—a leap away from the solid reality of rock and into the unknown.

Driven by your desperate trembling arms and your trust in the ancient carvings, you push away from the cliff. As your body passes through the waterfall, a sensation unlike any other envelops you. The rushing water crashes against your skin with a force that feels like being engulfed in a fierce, living embrace. The droplets dance around you, sparkling in the sunlight that filters through the cascading veil, creating a mesmerizing play of light and shadow.

Your heart pounds in your chest and your vision blurs as you plunge into the cascade, feeling as though you are being swallowed by a living creature of water and foam The turbulent rush of the waterfall surrounds you, pulling you downward with a fierce intensity. Your body tumbles and twists in the churning current, carried along by an irresistible force that seems both ancient and eternal.

As you emerge on the other side, a sense of profound connection washes over you. It feels like something ancient and powerful, stirring deep within your soul. The air rushes past you as you fall, the roar of the waterfall a deafening companion in your descent. The thrill of the leap mixes with a rising tide of fear as the cold spray of the waterfall envelopes you, the world beyond reduced to a blur of motion and sound.

Then, the impact—the water is shockingly cold, a liquid ice that wraps around you, stealing the breath from your lungs. You surface, gasping for air, the initial rush of adrenaline fading. Beneath you a light seems to pulse in the depths, could it be the Crystal of Destiny that you've been looking for?

As you dive deeper, drawn by a shifting glow that promises wonders, the true nature of the light becomes clear. It's not the Crystal of Destiny you had hoped for but a creature of the depths, its body aglow with a haunting light. Its beauty is undeniable, a living gem in the heart of the forest's waters, but it's a beauty laced with danger.

The creature moves with a purpose, its movements graceful yet terrifyingly quick. Before you can react, it's upon you, its embrace inescapable. You are pulled deeper, the light from above fading, replaced by the oppressive darkness of the depths. In this moment, as despair takes hold, the true cost of your actions becomes painfully clear.

The Enchanted Forest, with all its mysteries and wonders, demands respect—a respect you cast aside in your haste and hubris. Your pursuit of glory, driven by a desire to uncover the forest's secrets without heed to the warnings, has led you to this end. The creature of the deep, guardian of the very mysteries you sought to claim, becomes the instrument of your undoing.

As darkness claims you, a final realization crystallizes in your mind. The quest for the Crystal of Destiny was more than a test of bravery; it was a lesson in wisdom, humility, and respect for the natural world—a lesson learned too late. The forest reclaims what is its, leaving your tale as a caution to those who would follow, a stark reminder that the greatest dangers often lie hidden behind the lure of adventure and discovery. The moral of your story, etched into the very essence of the forest, is clear: bravery without wisdom is folly, and the pursuit of greatness, without consideration for the balance of nature, leads only to downfall.

The End

Continue fighting the creature.

With your weapon lost to the depths of the forest and the creature before you, a defiant spark ignites within your heart. Refusing to succumb to the creeping dread that fills the air, you charge at the creature, your fists raised, a primal scream tearing from your throat. The darkness around you seems to pulse with anticipation, the forest itself a silent observer to this desperate clash.

As you reach the creature, your fist connects with its body, but not with the solid impact you expected. Instead, your hand sinks into its flesh, squishy and cold, like punching into a dense fog made solid. Startled by the unexpected sensation, you attempt to pull back, but it's too late. The creature reacts quickly, its tentacles whipping out to ensnare you.

The tentacles are like chains, cold and unyielding, wrapping around you with an inevitability that leaves no room for escape. They coil around your limbs, pulling you closer to the creature, its body pulsating with a haunting light that now seems more like a warning than a beacon.

In a panic, you struggle against the creature's grip, but each movement only tightens its hold. With a swift, determined pull, the creature drags you beneath the surface of the water, the world above fading away as you're plunged into the cold, suffocating depths.

The water closes over you, a cold embrace that steals the warmth from your body and the air from your lungs. Your vision blurs as you sink deeper, the light from the creature leading you not to treasure but to the heart of an abyss you never intended to explore.

As the darkness claims you, a realization colder than the water seeps into your soul. The pursuit of the Crystal of Destiny, driven by a reckless bravery devoid of wisdom, has led you here. The forest, with all its ancient allure, commands a respect you failed to give, a lesson learned too late.

In the depths, your fate becomes a cautionary tale whispered by the trees of the Enchanted Forest. A warning of the dangers that lie in wait for those who seek power without humility, who face the darkness without light. The moral, as old as the forest itself, is clear: true bravery is not in the fight, but in knowing when to seek another way, understanding that some secrets are kept for a reason, and the cost of uncovering them can be greater than you're prepared to pay.

<u>The End</u>

Climb back down to solid ground.

With the decision made to return to solid ground, you face the cliff once more, your resolve mingling with a flicker of disappointment. The descent looms before you, a reversal of the perilous climb that brought you to the cave's shadowed entrance. The rocks, slick with the constant mist from the waterfall, seem to jeer at your caution, each one a treacherous step back into the world you momentarily left behind.

The journey downward is arduous. Your muscles scream in protest, a harsh reminder of the strain they've already endured. Each handhold and foothold is a gamble, the slippery surface offering little assurance of safety. Your breath comes in sharp gasps, the cold air biting at your lungs, as you navigate the treacherous path with painstaking care.

About halfway down, disaster strikes. Your foot, seeking a familiar crevice, finds only slick rock. Time slows as you slide, your heart thundering in your chest, a silent scream caught in your throat. By sheer instinct, your hands scrabble against the cliff face, seeking salvation. Miraculously, your left hand finds purchase, a jutting stone that bears your weight, but just barely.

Relief is short-lived. Moments later, your right hand slips, pebbles and small stones cascading down into the void below as a testament to your peril. Dangling precariously, supported by the strained fingers of your left hand, you feel the gravel beneath that fragile grip begin to shift, a silent countdown to a fall that promises nothing but despair.

Climb back up. (Go to page 86)

Continue climbing down. (Go to page 88)

Leap from the rock wall. (Go to page 78)

Climb back up.

With every ounce of determination, you decide to pull yourself back up to the depression in the cliff. It's not just a climb; it's a battle against exhaustion. Your arms ache with every movement, and your legs tremble as if they might give out at any moment. Yet, the fear of falling pushes you beyond your limits.

Gritting your teeth, you swing your arm back up, searching for any hold that might support your weight. Your fingers find a small ledge, barely enough to grip, but it suffices. Inch by painstaking inch, you haul yourself up, fighting against gravity and fatigue. When you finally drag yourself over the ledge, collapsing onto solid ground, relief washes over you. Exhausted yet triumphant, you've never felt so tired but victorious.

Deciding to brave the darkness and hoping you've interpreted the ancient poem's hidden messages correctly, you step into the cave's mouth. A chill envelops you as the light from outside dims, the cave swallowing you into its shadows. Mixed feelings of thrill and fear tingle down your spine as you venture into the unknown, your left hand reaching out to caress the smooth, damp cave wall that guides you deeper.

The cool touch of the rock and the sound of water droplets in the silence provide a soothing backdrop to the tension that tightens with every step forward. Then, a faint squelch breaks the monotony—something is moving in the darkness. As you move deeper, the noise grows louder, more defined, signaling another presence within the cave.

Your heart races, instincts screaming caution. Fear tightens its grip as the squelching grows closer, an ominous harbinger of what's to come. Frozen in place, you're torn between fleeing and facing the approaching menace. Then, a soft glow pierces the darkness, a pulsing light that draws nearer with each second. It's unsettling yet mesmerizing, compelling you to stay your ground.

As the source of the light comes into view, you're greeted by a sight both wondrous and strange. A creature, small and round, its body a glowing orb in the oppressive darkness, moves with ease, leaving a trail of bioluminescent light in its wake. Its form is like nothing you've seen before, a being of light in a world of shadow.

Follow the glowing creature. (Go to page 50)

Search the cave on your own. (Go to page 48)

Continue climbing down.

You carefully descend the cliff, your arms and legs straining under the relentless tug of gravity. This risky path, though perilous, promises the quickest route to safety. Your hand reaches out for another grip, fingers sliding across the cold, damp rock. Your muscles burn with exhaustion, demanding respite, yet you press on, reminding yourself to breathe and focus. Suddenly, your foot slips, sending a sharp wave of fear through your body. With a frantic effort, you stabilize yourself, your heart hammering in your chest.

However, the moment of relief is fleeting. As you search for a new foothold, disaster strikes without warning. Your hand loses its grip, and you are sent tumbling downward. Time seems to crawl as you fall, the earth rushing up to meet you.

The wind howls in your ears, muting all other sounds as the ground below merges into a blur of greens and browns. Adrenaline surges through you, your heart pounding with the rhythm of imminent danger. As you plummet, your clothes and hair flail wildly in the gusts of air.

Despite the terror, a bizarre calm overtakes you. You close your eyes momentarily, seeking to shut out the grim reality of the impact awaiting you. Rejecting panic, you focus on controlling your descent. Your eyes snap open; you twist your body, recalling tales of adventurers who maneuvered through peril by their wits.

Your last-second adjustments position you slightly better. You tuck your arms to shield your head, bracing for the collision. The impact, though severe, is not fatal. It forcefully expels the air from your lungs as you roll along the soft, damp underbrush, which absorbs some of the blow.

A sharp pain radiates through you, signaling the severity of your fall, yet you find yourself intact. As you lie on the forest floor, catching your breath, the reality of your survival dawns on you. The ordeal leaves you bruised and aching, yet unbroken.

Reflecting on the fall, you recognize it as a harsh lesson in caution, underscoring the need to respect the inherent dangers of adventure and the importance of learning from your errors. Slowly, you rise, the forest a verdant haze around you. Your journey continues, now with a deeper appreciation for the choices you make and the challenges they bring. This mishap becomes a chapter in your saga, reinforcing the possibility of recovery and growth even amidst fear and uncertainty.

Enter the dark cave. (Go to page 38)

Search the mist-shrouded pond. (Go to page 47)

Tuck and roll upon landing.

You launch into the air, and time stretches as you soar across the gap, adrenaline and the cold rush of air fueling your flight. Your heart beats in tandem with the sound of tumbling stones, creating a symphony of chaos as you aim for salvation.

As you land, instinct prompts you to roll across the rugged ground to soften the impact. The roll is rough, and sharp stones graze your skin, sending pain through your shoulder as it bears your weight. Despite the discomfort, you push onward, driven by the urgency to escape the turmoil behind you.

At the end of your roll, you rise from a cloud of dust into solid ground, aching but safe. Turning back, you see the ground where you landed has collapsed into a pit. A fresh breeze carrying the scent of flowers flows from the cave opening, promising sunlight and fresh air. With each step toward the exit, the cave's hold loosens, and you emerge into the sunlight, feeling its warmth against your back.

Pausing to catch your breath, you observe a vast field before you, with the cave's mouth interrupting the tranquil landscape. Nearby, a dense grove beckons, its branches weaving a dark canopy that invites exploration into its mysterious depths, hinting at hidden wonders and potential dangers.

To your left, a strikingly different scene unfolds: a manicured garden offers a serene escape. Bright flowers and a winding path lead to a softly glowing fountain and a solitary bench, creating a haven of peace. This garden, with its vibrant colors and calming sounds, provides a soothing space to recover from your recent ordeal, promising solace in nature's gentle embrace.

Between the wild allure of the grove and the tranquil beauty of the garden, you face a choice between the thrill of adventure and the peace of recovery. Each path offers a unique journey, reflecting the dual nature of your surroundings.

Explore the grove. (Go to page 96)

Explore the garden. (Go to page 98)

Brace for impact with your legs.

As you soar through the air, the gaping pit below a dizzying void, your heart races in your chest like a trapped animal. The far edge of the pit, your only hope for survival, looms closer with each passing moment, a thin thread of salvation amidst the all-consuming darkness of the cave.

You brace for impact, legs tense and ready to absorb the shock. Your determination is a shield, your confidence the spear that drives you forward. The edge looms, a promise of solid ground, a whisper of safety.

You land with a heavy thud, but the landing is far from the graceful, controlled stop you envisioned. The ground beneath your feet, crumbly and weak, betrays you. A heavy grinding noise fills the air, as the edge gives way beneath your weight.

You panic and scramble, but the earth continues to crumble, taking you with it. You slide back towards the darkness you so desperately sought to escape, the ground beneath you disappearing into the abyss.

Try to grab onto the remaining edge. (Go to page 93)

Attempt to leap forward. (Go to page 95)

Try to grab onto the remaining edge.

As the ground beneath you gives way, a desperate plan forms. Scrambling up shifting, unstable rocks, your hands claw at the earth, seeking anything to offer purchase in this chaotic descent. Your fingers brush against the edge, a fleeting hope surges through you. For a moment, you feel solid ground beneath your fingertips, a lifeline amidst chaos. But it's a cruel illusion; the edge crumbles at your touch, offering no support. As your fingers slip, the realization hits—there's no catching yourself. The darkness below rushes up to meet you, a gaping maw ready to swallow you whole. Panic and disbelief mingle as you plummet into the unknown. The fall is a blur, the air a cold whisper, the darkness a shroud that dims hope. Your descent is a stark lesson: bravery and determination must be tempered with caution. Courage without wisdom is perilous; true adventures demand strength, bravery, and respect for the unknown.

The End

Attempt to leap from the collapsing ground.

In a desperate move, you leap from a crumbling ledge. As the ground disintegrates, sending rocks and dust into the abyss, you propel yourself forward, adrenaline surging as time dilates around you. The cold air clashes with your frantic heartbeat, which mirrors the chaotic descent of the stones behind you.

The impact of landing is imminent. Recalling the ground's recent betrayal, you instinctively tuck your shoulder and execute a rough roll across the uneven terrain. The terrain scrapes at your skin, and a sharp pain spikes through your shoulder as it absorbs the impact. Grimacing but determined, you stifle a cry and persevere through the pain, driven by the urgency to flee the chaos.

Once on your feet, pain throbs through your body, but you push on towards the cave's exit, motivated by the beckoning sunlight and fresh air. With each step, the cave's hold weakens until you finally emerge into the daylight, its warmth contrasting starkly with the dark you've left behind.

Catching your breath, you survey your surroundings. You stand on the edge of a vast field, the cave's entrance marking the tranquil landscape. Before you, a grove stands as a wild testament to nature's untamed spirit. Its intertwined branches create a dense canopy, plunging the ground into twilight and radiating an energy that suggests secrets lurking in its shadows. The grove beckons, promising adventure and hidden wonders, calling to your inner explorer.

To your left, a manicured garden offers a stark contrast. Bright flowers and a winding path lead to a softly glowing fountain, where a bench invites rest and contemplation. This garden is a place of peace, designed to comfort the weary and satisfy the curious. With its vibrant blooms and soothing water sounds, the garden offers a place to recover from past dangers and enjoy a moment of peace, encapsulating the simple joys of nature's gentle embrace.

Faced with a choice between the mysterious grove and the tranquil garden, you contemplate the allure of adventure against the promise of peace, each path reflecting a unique facet of the surrounding wilderness.

Explore the grove. (Go to page 96)

Explore the garden. (Go to page 98)

Explore the grove.

After navigating the treacherous paths of the Enchanted Forest, facing its guardians, and learning from its secrets, you find yourself in an ancient grove, untouched by time. The air here is thick with magic, and the ground is a carpet of glowing moss, casting a soft glow around you. In the center of this grove stands an ancient tree, its branches reaching towards the sky like open arms, and its roots deep and sprawling, entwined with the very heart of the forest.

As you approach the tree, you notice a glimmer coming from the roots, nestled within a natural alcove. As you get closer, you see that it is the Crystal of Destiny, pulsing with a soft light that matches the glow of the luminescent moss on the ground. The moss-covered ground and surrounding trees seem to hum with energy in response to its presence. The air around the tree and the crystal is thick with the scent of fresh earth and growing plants, mixed with the faint aroma of something sweet and magical. The smell is invigorating, like a mixture of a summer rain shower and a garden in bloom. The crystal is a beautiful shade of emerald green, reflecting the colors of the enchanted forest around it. The crystal is not just a treasure to be taken—it's a part of the forest itself, a symbol of the balance between seeking one's desires and preserving the natural world.

As you draw closer to the crystalline core of the forest nestled within the roots of the ancient tree, it seems to pulse with gentle light that resonates with the very heartbeat of the woods. It is a precious treasure, yet also a vital piece of the forest's delicate equilibrium, a reminder of the delicate balance between chasing our desires and preserving the natural world. As you reach out to touch the crystal, you feel a slight tingling sensation in your fingertips. The surface of the crystal is smooth and cool to the touch, almost like glass. It feels like you are connecting with something ancient and powerful.

You consider taking the crystal may disrupt the balance of the forest, but could grant you unparalleled power but at the cost of the very magic and beauty that led you here. However, if you leave the crystal, you may be honoring the harmony of the forest. A choice that represents the understanding that some treasures hold more value when left undiscovered, safeguarding the enchantment of the Enchanted Forest for generations to come, but then what was the whole point of this journey?

Take the Crystal of Destiny. (Go to page 100)

Leave the Crystal where it is. (Go to page 102)

Explore the garden.

As you wander through the garden, the beauty around you is overwhelming. Flowers in hues you've never seen before line the winding path, their fragrances mingling in the air to create a perfume that's both exhilarating and calming. The gentle sound of the fountain, with water sparkling under the soft glow, invites you closer, promising a moment of peace after your harrowing escape.

Drawn to the center of the garden, you discover a mound of earth and moss, so inviting in its softness. It seems like the perfect place to rest, a natural bed crafted by the garden itself. The exhaustion from your journey weighs heavily on your limbs, and the serene sound of the fountain, combined with the sweet scent of the flowers, lulls you into a sense of security. Without a second thought, you lay down, feeling the soft moss cushion your body. Your eyelids grow heavy, and you surrender to the peaceful slumber that beckons.

But peace turns to terror in an instant. Just as you drift into sleep, the ground beside you erupts. Two skeletal arms, cold and unyielding, shoot out of the earth on either side of you. Their grasp is chilling, a stark contrast to the warmth of the garden. Panic surges through you as the skeleton's icy fingers wrap around your arms, pulling you toward the ground.

You fight against the skeletal arms with all your might, but the grip is too strong. With a sudden jolt, you are pulled under the ground, the earth closing in around you like a hungry mouth. Darkness envelops you, and the sensation of being buried alive sends shivers down your spine.

As you struggle to free yourself as dirt tumbles on top of you, weighing you down with its suffocating pressure. The earth presses against your chest, making it hard to breathe. Panic rises within you like a tidal wave, threatening to consume you whole as the last of the light disappears in a cascade of dirt.

The End

Take the Crystal of Destiny.

With the weight of your decision heavy in the air, you reach out and carefully remove the Crystal of Destiny from its ancient resting place among the roots of the towering tree. As your fingers brush against its surface, a surge of energy courses through you, a torrent of power that floods your senses with visions.

The crystal, pulsing with a light as old as the forest itself, connects you to a future you had only dared to imagine. Images flash before your eyes, vivid and commanding. You see yourself returning to Meadowfen, your home, a hero's welcome awaiting you. The villagers gather, their faces alight with awe and admiration as you share tales of your journey and the discovery of the crystal.

As the power of prophecy fills your being, you foresee wealth and prosperity flowing into your life, a reward for your courage and determination. But with this gift comes a shadow, a darkness that creeps at the edges of your vision. The forest, once a source of mystery and adventure, becomes a place of fear and suspicion for the villagers. Its magic, disrupted by the crystal's absence, twists into something unrecognizable, a stark reminder of the cost of your choice.

A jealousy, sharp and insidious, takes root in your heart, the crystal's power a siren call that you cannot ignore.

You see yourself pulling away from friends and loved ones, their intentions suspect in your eyes. The fear that they might seek to claim the crystal's power for themselves grows until it colors every interaction, every shared moment.

Despite the warning in your visions, the desire to return the crystal, to undo the choice that has brought you here, flickers weakly in your resolve. The allure of the power you now hold, the potential for greatness, overshadows the creeping doubts and the knowledge of what might be lost.

In the end, you take the crystal back to Meadowfen, the visions you experienced unfolding into reality. Your newfound status brings you everything you thought you wanted, but the cost is high. The forest at the edge of the village, once a place of wonder and exploration, becomes a boundary, a dark reminder of the price of power.

The End

Leave the Crystal where it is.

As you stand before the ancient tree, its roots cradling the Crystal of Destiny like a precious child, a wave of understanding washes over you. The crystal's glow, mesmerizing and full of untold power, beckons, but deep within, you feel a stirring of respect for the balance of the forest. With a heavy heart but a clear mind, you step back, leaving the crystal untouched. It is a decision that honors the harmony of the Enchanted Forest, recognizing that some treasures are meant to remain secrets, their true value lying in the balance they maintain.

As you retreat, the air around you shifts, the atmosphere charged with a sense of ancient magic. From the very heart of the tree, a guardian emerges, its form ethereal and awe-inspiring, woven from the light and shadows of the forest itself. The guardian's eyes meet yours, and in that gaze, you feel a deep, unspoken gratitude for the choice you've made.

In recognition of your respect and wisdom, the guardian grants you a boon—a seed from the very essence of the Enchanted Forest. This is no ordinary seed, but one imbued with the magic of growth and healing, capable of bringing prosperity and harmony to the land it touches.

With the guardian's gift secured, you return to your village of Meadowfen, the weight of the crystal's temptation no longer on your shoulders. Instead, you carry with you the promise of a brighter future, one that you will cultivate with the magic seed.

Planting the seed in the heart of the village, you watch in wonder as it takes root, sprouting and growing at a miraculous pace. The magic within the seed spreads, enriching the soil, making the crops flourish like never before, and filling the air with the sweet scent of endless blossoms. The once modest village of Meadowfen transforms into a haven of abundance and beauty, a testament to the harmony between humanity and the natural world.

Your friends and fellow villagers gather, their faces alight with joy and wonder at the transformation you've brought about. Celebrated not just for the prosperity you've ushered in but for the wisdom of your choice, you grow to be an important figure in Meadowfen. Your decision to leave the Crystal of Destiny untouched becomes a tale told through generations, a story of respect for the unknown and the power of thoughtful choices.

In choosing to honor the forest and its secrets, you've found a different kind of power—the ability to bring about real change and happiness. The Enchanted Forest remains a place of mystery and magic at the edge of Meadowfen, its balance preserved, while the village thrives under the watchful gaze of the trees. Your story, a bridge between two worlds, serves as a reminder that true strength lies in understanding and respect, and that sometimes, the greatest treasures are those we choose not to take.

The End

Ask about the skeleton.

In the tranquil clearing, the old man turns to you, his eyes reflecting the wisdom of years spent in solitude, guarding secrets known only to the forest. "The path ahead," he begins, his voice low and steady, "is fraught with challenges that will test you in ways you can't yet imagine. It's a journey that demands more than mere strength and bravery. To find what you truly seek within Eldoria, you'll need wisdom, insight, and the courage to make difficult choices."

He gestures towards the stone pillar standing solemnly amongst the trees, its surface etched with carvings that seem to dance in the flickering light of the fireflies. "Every great adventure," he continues, "begins with a choice. The path you choose to walk, the tools you decide to carry—these will shape your journey, your destiny."

His gaze shifts to the rusty sword and the faded note, clutched in the skeleton's bony grasp. "Tools," he says, "can be more than they appear. They can open paths, reveal secrets, or close doors forever." His voice carries a cryptic note, hinting at deeper truths. "One might offer you the strength to confront your foes head-on, to carve your way through obstacles with the might of your arm. The other could unlock mysteries, offer insights whispered only in the silent language of magic. But remember, not everything is as it seems in the heart of Eldoria."

The old man's eyes meet yours, a spark of challenge within their depths. "Choosing one," he suggests, his tone laced with subtext, "will define not just your journey but who you become. Will you take up the sword, become a warrior in a land that respects the strength of arms? Or will you unfold the parchment, seek the wisdom that comes from understanding the mysteries of the world?"

His words hang in the air, heavy with implication. The sword and the parchment lie before you, symbols of diverging paths on your adventure. The old man's advice, though shrouded in mystery, guides you towards a choice that resonates with the core of your being.

In this moment of decision, the lesson is clear: your journey through Eldoria will be shaped by the choices you make, and the tools you choose to aid you. Whether through the strength or the insight, the path to discovering what you seek requires more than meets the eye.

Investigate the pillar. (Go to page 17)

Investigate the skeleton. (Go to page 20)

Take the sword.

You carefully reach out and grab the sword the skeleton is holding. As your fingers touch the hilt, the sudden movement causes the old piece of parchment in the skeleton's other hand to fall to the ground. The paper crumbles into several pieces, turning into a puzzle you can no longer solve. You feel a bit sad about it, but your attention quickly shifts back to the sword.

The moment the sword is fully in your grip, it begins to vibrate, sending a strange, tingling feeling through your arm. You try to let go, scared by the unexpected power, but your hand won't listen. Just as you start to panic, the vibration stops, and the feeling turns comforting, almost like it's making you stronger. You swing the sword through the air, amazed at how natural and right it feels in your hand. Unhooking the scabbard from around the skeleton's waist, you wrap it around your own, the sword sliding into place as if it had always belonged there.

The skeleton stands up, its empty eye sockets staring at you. With a clattering of bones, it lunges forward, attacking you! You quickly draw the sword and block the first strike. Feeling the weight of the sword in your hand, you swing at the skeleton. The battle is fierce. The skeleton swings its bony arms at you, and you dodge and parry with all your might. You slash at its ribcage. The skeleton stumbles but keeps coming. You step back and take a deep breath, then charge forward, swinging the sword with all your strength. The blade slices through the skeleton's spine, and it collapses into a pile of bones at your feet.

Breathing heavily, you look at the remains of your foe. The thrill of victory is quickly replaced by a memory of the brigands who have been harassing the people of Meadowfen. You decide to return home to defend your village, abandoning your quest for the Crystal of Destiny.

Back in Meadowfen, the villagers are overjoyed. With the enchanted sword in your hand, you lead the charge against the brigands, fighting bravely and skillfully. The brigands are swiftly defeated, and the people of Meadowfen celebrate your heroism. As you bask in the admiration of your fellow villagers, you often wonder what would have happened if you had continued searching for the crystal.

The End

If you're unhappy with this ending, go to page 24 of

Whispers of the Eldroian Crystal:

The Path of the Warrior

to continue your journey.

You reach down and gently take the note from the skeleton's grasp. The paper feels brittle under your fingers, as if it might crumble at any moment. You unfold it carefully, and the words on the page begin to shimmer with a mysterious blue light. Before you can react, the note bursts into a cascade of blue sparks, disintegrating right before your eyes. A wave of energy sweeps through you, tingling and vibrant. It's as if the forest itself is whispering secrets directly into your mind, filling you with arcane knowledge.

In the midst of this whirlwind of sensations, a soft, ethereal voice whispers in your head, revealing secrets of magic hidden within the forest. Your heart races with excitement as you realize you're being gifted ancient wisdom.

As the last of the blue light fades, a thick book with a sturdy leather cover appears out of thin air, landing softly in the underbrush at your feet. You pick it up, marveling at its sudden appearance, and begin to leaf through the pages. Inside, you find spells and incantations, symbols and words that should be foreign to you,

but instead, they resonate with a deep understanding. There's a spell to create a glowing orb of light, another to move objects without touching them, and many more, each with its own purpose and power.

Just as you're absorbing the wonder of the magical book and the spells it contains, an unexpected chill runs down your spine. The air in the clearing shifts, growing colder, denser. You look up—the skeleton, which moments ago was nothing more than bones and dust, is stirring, rising to its feet with an eerie grace. In its hand, the rusty sword now gleams with a sinister light, as if reawakened along with its owner.

The skeleton turns toward you, its empty sockets seeming to focus with an unnatural intelligence. With a sudden, jerky movement, it raises the sword and swings it at you with startling speed. You jump back just in time. The sword slices through the air where you stood, missing you by inches. The sound of it cutting through the air is a harsh whisper, a promise of danger.

Summoning your courage and the newfound magic flowing through you, you quickly raise your hand and chant a spell from the ancient book. A bright, crackling light bursts from your fingertips, striking the skeleton. The magic engulfs the skeletal figure, causing it to shudder violently before collapsing into a heap of bones and dust once more. The eerie glow of the sword fades, and the clearing falls silent.

Breathing heavily, you realize the power you now possess and the responsibility it brings. The thrill of adventure and the dangers of the forest weigh heavily on your mind. Deciding to use your newfound abilities for good, you make the choice to return to Meadowfen.

With the magical book securely in your grasp, you journey back to your village. There, you help the people of Meadowfen with your powers, healing the sick, aiding with harvests, and protecting them from harm. The villagers look up to you, grateful for your wisdom and strength.

Yet, as you settle into your new role, a part of you always wonders about the mysteries you left behind in the forest. Despite this, you find contentment in knowing that you made a difference in the lives of those you care about. The end.

The End

If you're unhappy with this ending, go to page 26 of
Whispers of the Eldroian Crystal:
The Path of the Mage
to continue your journey.

I hope you enjoyed your time in the Enchanted Forest of Eldoria in the *Path of the Commoner.* If you want more, check out the two companion books in the series:

Until then, sign up for my mailing list so you don't miss the updates, and get access to the official online version of

DREAMWEAVER DIARIES UNLOCKED

~ AN ORIGINAL ~

PICK·YOUR·PATH·ADVENTURE

www.ericjohnsonwriter.com

BOOKS BY ERIC JOHNSON

Dreamweaver Diaries

Book 1: Under the Shadow's Eye

Book 2: Depths of the Rebels' Stone

Book 3: Crossing Lines *(Coming Soon)*

The Second Coming

Book 1: The Lost

Poetry

The Conditions We Live

Transitions: A Story in Verse

Pick•Your•Path•Adventures

Unlocked (Dreamweaver Diaries Prequel)

Whispers of the Eldorian Crystal: Path of the Commoner

Whispers of the Eldorian Crystal: Path of the Warrior

Whispers of the Eldorian Crystal: Path of the Mage

ABOUT THE AUTHOR

In a home hidden among the woods, Eric Johnson finds his muse in the quiet hours of night and the lively adventures of day.

His writing journey reflects this blend. The Dreamweaver Diaries series, with titles like *Under the Shadow's Eye* and *Depths of the Rebels' Stone*, showcases his knack for weaving fantastical tales.

His poetic side is revealed in collections such as *The Conditions We Live* and *Transitions: A Story in Verse*, published by Unsolicited Press, where words paint vivid emotional landscapes.

When he's not guiding young minds or chasing after his own children, Eric is often found climbing trees, hiking in the forest, or lost in a book. His love for coffee, dark and rich, or something a bit stronger, mirrors his passion for storytelling.

For more about Eric's work and to join a community of readers, visit ericjohnsonwriter.com. Sign up for updates on new adventures in writing and life.